The
FRAGRANT MINUTE

FOR EVERY DAY

Wilhelmina
Stitch

"FOR HOPE SHALL BRIGHTEN DAYS TO COME,
AND MEMORY GILD THE PAST."
THOMAS MOORE

DAILY GRAPHIC—SERIES NO. 1

The Fragrant
Minute for Every Day

Wilhelmina Stitch

The
FRAGRANT MINUTE
FOR EVERY DAY.

Wilhelmina
Stitch

"FOR HOPE SHALL BRIGHTEN DAYS TO COME,
AND MEMORY GILD THE PAST."
THOMAS·MOORE

INTRODUCTION

N o one pretends that it is a poetical gift alone which has brought such swift and widespread popularity to Wilhelmina Stitch. Her homely little verses, which appear day by day in the Daily Graphic, have touched the hearts of innumerable men and women because of the spirit of helpfulness which pervades them, and the charming, joyous personality they reveal. The simple virtues, implanted deep in the human soul, are what they exalt — courage, kindliness, gratitude, faith, love and loyalty.

Most of us are of common clay. We only desire to walk in seemly paths, and live serenely. It may be that Wilhelmina Stitch recovers for us the glamour of half-forgotten days, the sweetness of memories, the buoyancy of childhood. It may be that she reminds us of something fragrant within ourselves of which contact with life is prone to rob us.

Whatever her charm may be, it is true and imperishable. If these few examples of her smiling philosophy, and those which follow them in the Daily Graphic, bring ease where it is wanted, and courage where it is lacking, they will more than serve their purpose.

TO F. C.

I will make rhymes for your delight, soft songs to usher in the night, and verses to be read at morn to greet the day so newly born. My words will be like shining beads; like little, loving, tender deeds; I'll string them on a golden thread, a circlet from a Fairy's head. O take my string of little words, and some will sweetly sing like birds, and some will twinkle just like stars, and some burn steadily, like Mars. O take my little rippling rhymes, for some will have the sound of chimes, and some will have life's beat and throb, and some a laugh, and some a sob, and some like helpful hands will be outstretched to you in sympathy; and some may even have the charms of warm, encircling, tender arms! I will make rhymes for your delight; like little stars they'll shine at night; by day, they'll work a magic charm to keep our love quite safe from harm.

WILHELMINA STITCH.

First Day

THE HAPPIEST AGE

hat age is happiest? Had you asked me, I would have made this plea: the *Now* is best. What joy to live with zest each newborn day; and from the Moment wrest what Life will give away. The Past is but a guest who came and went, and left this one behest: to be content.

Think how To-day is blest! We've eyes to see Nature in Beauty drest for you, for me. What matter that the crest of Youth is past. Youth lives within the breast with joys that last. The will to do our best, and hands for giving. Oh! *Now*'s the happiest, best time for living!

What age is happiest? Oh! hear my vow, for I have put the test—the happiest's *Now*. Sweet sighs and kindly jest for warmth and cheer; and Love's most high bequest to crown the year.

Second Day

MY HOUSE

I'll build my house of cotton-wool; 'twill take at least, three big bags full. I'll sprinkle it with dust o' stars, six pints from Vega, six from Mars; then in the night, my friends will see my house a-twinkling merrily!

I'll have no chairs, nor yet a bed, but mounds of thistle-down instead. My cup will be a horn-like shell that secret of the sea can tell. A shell of pink will be my plate; its flutings will foretell my fate. I'll eat the sweetness from the air and sip the wine from blossoms rare. I'll clothe myself in magic weaves of petals white, and bright green leaves.

My mother will be Queen of Snow; my father, King of Firelight Glow. At night with gnomes I'll gaily dance beneath the moon's aloof pale glance, and I will sweetly talk, at dawn, with many a friendly Leprechaun.

And sometimes, Memories will be—my guests for breakfast, luncheon, tea!

Third Day

FIRESIDE THOUGHTS

hat is more lovely, think you, than a fire, with dark, mysterious hills blacker than night, through which a cavern, like a great desire, glows golden red, its walls with gems bedight? And flames, like sprites so tantalizing, bold, flirt with these hilltops, daring, debonair; now blue, now red, now robed in flaunting gold, they flicker, bend, and leap into the air!

What is more lovely than a fire, think you, awaiting one who treads the homeward way, beaming its welcome, comforting and true, to Weary Worker at the close of day? I am much humbled when I think of fires which warm the spirit as they warm the hand, and with no questioning of our desires, commune in silence, commune and understand.

What is more lovely than a fire that leaps at Mother's rings and Baby's wriggling toes, and joins the laughter till the baby sleeps, and then sleeps, too—a full-blown, grey-rimmed rose?

Fourth Day

AMBITIONS

We were sitting near the fire (Oh! the birchwood flames were gold, and the birchwood flames were bold) and each spoke of her desire. There was Joyce, impetuous Joyce (Oh! the birchwood flames turned blue, and the birchwood bark burned through), as she spoke in thrilling voice, "I so wish I were a man (Oh! the birchwood flames flared high and the birch-logs seemed to sigh) then I'd travel for a span."

Then another joined the throng (now the birch flames kept still, as if conquered by the will of this woman brave and strong). "Ah! my joy," she said, "would be" (then the birch-log split in twain, showed its heart a-fire with pain), "to be turned into a tree. A tree with kindly graces, a tree that makes cool places for a traveller worn and weary of Life's desert road so dreary. Indeed, I'd love to be (said this much-loved friend to me) a comforting and shady, and a stately, wide-branched tree!"

Fifth Day

FRIENDSHIP

As wind to the lagging sail, as joy to the fleeting hour, as a staff to the weak and frail, as rain to the panting flow'r; as sun to the earth's cold breast, as bread to the hungry man, as sleep to those needing rest, as thought to the half-formed plan; as warmth to the poorly clad, as sky to the weary eye, as song to the old and sad, as wings to the birds that fly; as words to a lovely song, as memories sweet to the old, as conflict is to the strong, and the rays of the sun to the cold; as trees to the nesting bird, as light to the ship out at sea, as voice to the tender word—is the meaning of Friendship to me.

Sixth Day

SPARKS

I heard her say, as she bent low, "This log won't burn, I told you so. It needs another log, you see, to make it burn right merrily." I looked and saw the flames leap out and wrap the new log round about; so bright and vigorous the fire, just like a newborn, strong desire.

I thought: how like those logs are we, responsive to warm sympathy; just ashes if we have no friend with whom the heart and mind can blend. One minute, cheerless, almost dead, and then a word or two is said, and lo! forthwith a bright fire shines and life is filled with magic signs! When wood strikes wood there is a spark which flashes through the gloomiest dark. "A spark is light, and light is truth," thus said a loved one in my youth.

And so it is when heart strikes heart, a fire is kindled, flames upstart. The log, it cannot burn alone; the heart, untouched, is cold as stone.

Seventh Day

THE ARCHITECT

B" uild me a house," my little laddie said (Oh! how resist the pleading of those eyes?), "a big, tall house, with chair and little bed. Please, mummie, do, a house of 'normous size."

And so I sat beside him on the floor and built a house with his gay-coloured blocks. Of cardboard were the windows and the door, and pins were used for handles and for locks. My little son then clapped his hands with glee, and round my neck his eager arms he flung. "Oh! what a lovely house you've built for me!" His praise was like a song that's sweetly sung.

But when I tucked him up in bed that night, caressed his curls, and kissed his fragrant face, a shadow fell upon my day's delight—and in my heart that shadow found a place.

How can I build for you, my little son; how can I build for you the House of Life; when once your childhood days are o'er and done, how can I build against the storm and strife? The strong foundation, yes, so much I can—but you must build Life's House from your own plan.

Eighth Day

WEALTH

In your pocket little cash, not enough to make a splash, not enough to buy a car, nor a pearl and diamond star. In your heart there's sunshine bright, queerest feelings of delight; feelings, too, of strength and health, better far than all the wealth.

In your home no Persian rugs, nor Venetian cut-glass jugs; the only heirloom in the house, a little midnight scuttling mouse! In your heart, Oh, treasures rare, golden dreams and visions fair, heirlooms from one's childhood days—flowers, and pictures, lilting lays.

Men so often lose their gold (then possessions must be sold); rarest Persian rugs aren't worth happiness, contentment, mirth. Hold thou fast, Oh, heart of mine, to the joy one can't define. To the joy that makes Life seem ... just as lovely as a Dream.

Ninth Day

AN ACT OF GRACE

ome folks perform such acts of grace; it makes one's heart leap up and sing; the world becomes a beauteous place, and one can dance like anything! I saw ('twas but the other day) how folks a-living on one street had all decided they would pay to give a poorer lad a treat.

Oh! not a treat to rouse his mirth, nor yet a dinner hot and choice, but something precious, of great worth—they'd pay to train his gifted voice.

Oh, Singing Lad! Unmoneyed Lad! They would not let his gift be lost, for such a voice might well make glad souls that were tired and tempest-tossed.

I have a vision of this boy returning on swift, eager feet, and lifting up his voice in joy to sing to that great-hearted street. And every door will open wide and every window upward go, and all the folks that are inside will smile to hear the lad they know!

Tenth Day

MY BANK

I'm hoarding for my ripe old age, a bankrupt I refuse to be. Oh, I am canny, cool, and sage—my method's good, you will agree. I'm hoarding memories of fun, of joyous days when hearts beat high, of hours of ease when work was done, and rosy was the western sky.

There is a bank within my heart; there is a bank within my mind; at finance I am very smart—I'm hoarding gentle words and kind! I'm saving lovely sights I've seen and lovely sounds my ears have heard: the trees bedecked in Springtime green, the song of human voice and bird. And grains of courage I invest; I'll draw upon them in my need. Old age is sometimes sore depressed, this Courage will my spirit feed.

I saw a poster yesterday that urged great thrift each youthful hour. I'll bank a cheerful thought each day—so my old age won't turn me sour!

Eleventh Day

WEE CLOTHES

 ee clothes, wee clothes, see them in a store; cunning things, tiny things, I just adore! Softest things, warmest things, dainty and white—to touch them, to feel them, gives keen delight!

Scotland sent blankets, soft as kitten's fur, cosiest of shawls—see the Baby stir! France sent dresses, billowy with lace, winsomest of dresses for His Tiny Grace. England sent bootees, knitted all by hand, white, blue, and pink ones, such a merry band. Switzerland sent ribbons, yards and yards of joy, pink for the new girl, and blue for the boy!

Wee clothes, wee clothes, once were in a store; now they have left it, left for evermore. In a handsome basket, see where they lie, awaiting the hours when great Storks fly! Wee clothes, wee clothes, see their charming pride, for now they've a baby, a sweet one, inside! The store—it was honest, the basket did not pall; but Wee Clothes are thinking that Baby's best of all!

Twelfth Day

THE "LADY BABY"

"On Nov. 14 the wife of——gave to the world a dear little lady baby."—Birth Announcement.

" Lady Baby came to-day." What words are quite so nice to say? They make one smile, they make one pray for Lady Baby's happiness. "To-day a Lady Baby came." We have not heard her winsome name, we can address her all the same, as Lady Baby-Come-to-Bless.

When Lady Baby came to earth, her home was filled with joy and mirth. There's not a jewel of half the worth of Lady Baby-To-Caress. We're glad that Lady Baby's here, for at this sunless time of year there's nought that brings such warmth and cheer as Lady Baby's daintiness.

Hush! Lady Baby's fast asleep, the friendly fire-flames dance and leap and angel's wings above her sweep as on her eyes a kiss they press. "A Lady Baby!" Lovely phrase, it means she'll have such gentle ways, and grow to goodness all her days—may God this Lady Baby bless!

Thirteenth Day

KEEP MOVING

I scanned wise words in a book to-day; this was the message, they seemed to say: Keep moving ahead! You can't stand still unless you really are very ill; for if you stop, like an unwound clock, you're bound to suffer a fearful shock, for something will happen to give you a shake, and say to your conscience, "Move on, awake."

Keep moving ahead, or your soul will die, and beauty evade your heart and eye. No matter at all that your pace be slow so long as you upward, upward go, into a finer atmosphere, where ideals live and visions clear, and Goodness and Truth have taken firm stand, and folks to folks stretch a loving hand.

For this be the measure of our success, the measure of all life's happiness: just how well we have moved ahead; or just how early our soul was dead!

Fourteenth Day

A THANKSGIVING

T o each his song of thankfulness; each heart its song of praise; and some will think of fertile fields, of golden wheat and maize; and some will think of clinking gold, of solid pompous wealth; and some will think of Love's high gift, and some will think of health.

But this my song of thankfulness, and this my song of praise—thank God for all the friendly books, for every magic phrase; for all the clever laughing books; for books that make one weep; for books one reads to little folks that they may sweetly sleep.

To each his song of thankfulness; for me this song of praise—thank God for all the lilting books, the rhythmic, glowing lays; for all the rich romantic books; for books like gentle hands; for books that take us on winged words to spirit-healing lands!

Fifteenth Day

DREAM SHIPS

O h! where do all the Dream Ships go, the ships that bravely went to sea in happy days of long ago, when hearts fared forth courageously?

You must go somewhere, little ships. And while we wait for your return we grow so tired, so cold our lips, the flame of life doth weakly burn.

I launched my Dream Ship with a splash, I laughed to see the waves leap high—the heart of Youth is ever rash—I gaily waved a pleased Good-bye. I said, "Next year my ship will sail into my waiting harbour-heart." Alas! my little ship was frail and failed to reach fair Dreamland's mart.

Each night I walked along the shore and looked at Neptune's wide domain; the circling gulls shrieked, "Never more! Your Dream Ship comes not back again."

"We'll look no more," said Weary Eyes. Said Weary Heart, "Those gulls spoke true." And then, to my intense surprise—my little ship sailed into view!

Sixteenth Day

ON 'BUS 15

hat a day! said I to me. The sky's as grey as it can be. The fog is really growing worse. To think I have to write a verse! There's not a thing to rhyme about—such drabness puts all thoughts to rout.

What fine balloons! So big and bright. The golden one is still in sight. Oh! see that pretty, tiny stall aglow with oranges and all. How lovely! Shining through the gloom, a flower-girl's basket rich with bloom. Despite the mist, the pigeons feed. A jolly sight it is, indeed, on such a very dreary day to see their grace and movements gay.

A solemn voice. "Your ticket, please." I prop my handbag on my knees and pull out trifles by the score. Then find it—lying on the floor. I laughed. He laughed. He scratched his head. "You women are a joke," he said. We talked a bit, and then I thought I've found the very thing I sought. I'll sketch this ride—where is my quill?—from Paddington to Ludgate-hill!

Seventeenth Day

FIGHTING FEARS

e stood our fears up one by one; we stood our fears up in a row, and then we had the greatest fun—we knocked them down with one sure blow. We aimed at them; in turn we aimed. We treated them like ninepins small; as each one fell, our courage flamed. Why, fears are nothing, after all!

When all were lying flat and dead, we looked into each other's eyes; we smiled, and both together said, "Those fears were just a pack of lies." We took them by their useless feet; I carried eight, he carried eight; we flung them on the dusty street, and there we left them to their fate.

And then before the fire we sat. Said I, "You are a splendid shot!" Said he, "You helped to knock them flat, and now we've killed the tiresome lot."

"I've gulped down fears," I said to him. "I've locked them up in cupboards, too. And one that was extremely grim was chained to me a whole year through. But, oh! this way was far the best—because we now can live with zest."

Eighteenth Day

SPILT MILK

O" h! what a pity!" pallid lips oft say. "If only we could wipe away that deed!" But Heart-of-Courage has another way, and for past failures does not pale nor bleed. I acted stupidly, a great mistake. Ah! well, I see it now, and will not weep nor whine; nor with remorse at night lie wide awake; nor with remorse by day, droop, peak and pine.

Mistakes are ever in the past, you see, we all of us can make a fresh, true start. I have no palate for despondency. I much revere the brave, the fighting heart. Oh! look not backwards, start just where you stand, we all of us can start our life anew: to fresh endeavour bring a willing hand, a spirit that will see the matter through.

You made mistakes? Dear sister, so did I. We'll make them yet again, of course we will. What matter failures, providing that we try to shape our life to goodness out of ill. Be not downhearted. To-day is on the wing and soon will be a portion of the past. To-morrow is the best of everything. To-morrow we'll succeed, quite well—at last!

Nineteenth Day

LITTLE PLANT-LOVERS

O h, you who to the parks did go, to share the plants they gave away, somehow I think I really know exactly how you felt that day. I saw you standing in a queue, impatient, eager, girls and boys. And truly, then, I shared with you, your great anticipated joys!

Oh, sweets are nice, of course they are! And so are toys, I quite agree; but certain things are nicer far—the blossoms that next spring you'll see, I think these were the thoughts you had as home you scurried, wreathed in smiles: "Now, won't these plants make Mother glad! what flowers we'll grow—just miles on miles!"

'Twas then a little prayer did flow from out my heart (it was for you) to Him who makes the flowers to grow and sends the sun and rain and dew. "O let their plants"—this was my plea—"take root and put forth blossoms fair. Then this good truth each child will see: in Beauty everyone may share!"

Twentieth Day

JACK AND JILL

ack and Jill went up the hill—the Hill of Life—together. And luck was good and luck was ill, and fair and foul the weather. It happened sometimes Jack fell down; but they were parted never, for Jill with love would mend his crown—ah, Jill was very clever!

Oh, Jack and Jill went up the hill—the Hill of Life—together; the smooth, the rough, each dale and vale, and they were parted never. It happened sometimes they would spill the bread and water life demands. Then Jack would smile, and so would Jill, and clasp in love each other's hands.

When both were old and both were grey, they reached the summit of Life's hill. Said they, "Life's been both work and play; and must be so for Jack and Jill."

And thus I read the dear old rhyme of Jack and Jill and water pail: the hurt is healed, yes, every time, if love betwixt them never fail.

Twenty-First Day

A PRAYER

 " ord, make us brave," I heard her say, and, looking up, I caught her eye. "Yes, brave," cried she, "to tread the way with cheerfulness until we die." "It's not much use," said she to me, "to live, unless we can be brave. For else we might go bitterly all our vexed hours, right to the grave."

It's only courage makes worth while this curious muddle we call life; to hearten others with a smile and lessen somewhat pain and strife.

"Lord, make us brave!" Oh! lovely phrase—I hear it ringing in my ears; a re-occurring song of praise that strengthens, uplifts, cheers. I think when troubles gather fast, or when my sun begins to set, "Lord, make me brave unto the last!" will be the words I'll ne'er forget.

Twenty-Second Day

ALONG THE WAY

" ather ye rosebuds while ye may," a pessimistic poet sang. Sweet joy, warned he, lives but a day; thus mournfully his verses rang. "Gather ye rosebuds while ye can"—O poet, dead these many years, yours was a wise and human plan, but born of vain and foolish fears.

The rosebuds droop, but other flowers spring up for us to pluck and twine into our calm, maturer hours—not youth alone knows love's red wine. And when the rosebuds are all dead, we'll see perchance a sturdier bloom, and pluck *that* for our joy instead, and find it, too, can banish gloom.

For every season brings to birth a flower for its own special joy. What would a rose-strewn life be worth without a thorn for its alloy? For every mile along the road, close to my hand a flow'r I'll find. I'll add its beauty to my load—and thank Old Time, the gardener kind.

Twenty-Third Day

BOTTOM DRAWER

Open it gently, look you inside. Garments so dainty, made for a bride. Silk things that shimmer, finest of lace, rosettes and ribbons to add to their grace.

Open it gently, what a sweet scent, perfumes from roses and lilies are blent. Garments so filmy, shell pink and white, Love's handiwork for a lover's delight. House linens also, here you may see, dear to the heart of a Bride-Soon-To-Be. Quaint things and lucky, gifts from her friends; close the drawer gently, inspection now ends!

Saw you the Dreams that hid in each fold, rose-tinted Dreams with circlets of gold? Saw you the Hopes with fairy-like wings, nestling with joy in Bride-To-Be's things? Saw you the Visions the Girl laid away, tender and true, with her Bridal array? Saw you the prayer I let slip inside—May God smile upon you, Soon-To-Be Bride!

Twenty-Fourth Day

THE WILL TO TRY

T o be content is not my rôle. I have not got a patient soul. I do not like to sit and wait in meek and mild and hopeful state.

Here is a door fast closed, I see; I wish 'twould open wide for me! I try a gentle knock or two; oh! door, I beg you, let me through. The door just shows a grim dark face: shall I sit down and wait a pace? Indeed, I won't, I'll knock again, and this time swift and sharp like rain. Indifferent and callous door, I'll bang again, and more and more!

My patient friends smile as they stand and see my bruised and bleeding hand. "You'll knock your head against a wall, that's what you'll do, and that is all. Just be content to stand outside, the world is very large and wide. That door is closed, just wait your turn, and don't with such impatience burn." But, oh! I'd rather, bleeding, die— than live without the will to try!

Twenty-Fifth Day

TO ONE BEREAVED

How beautiful a thing you made of life! And, think you, Sad-of-Heart, such Beauty goes? There is an end to ugliness and strife, but Love dies not, nor withers like the rose. Think of the Beauty that you found, you two. You through her soul and she through your own eyes. Saw you not Love, as year by year it grew, forging with strength its everlasting ties?

So when you feel your hurt too deep to bear, sweet memories will claim you for their own; create for you a vision passing fair—by it companioned, you are not alone. Oh! you who made of life a beauteous thing, know this to comfort you in darkened days, this truth to which the grieving heart may cling: she is alive in many lovely ways.

In every soothing sound, her voice you'll hear; wherever beauty is, you'll see her face; go where you will, you'll feel her spirit near—for in your heart she found her resting-place.

Twenty-Sixth Day

HOME-KEEPING

h" ome-keeping hearts are happiest!" 'Twas thus I heard a woman say as I walked swiftly to the west when going to my work to-day. A lovely phrase, I thought with zest, repeating it beneath my breath, "Home-keeping hearts are happiest," such magic words might vanquish death.

"Home-keeping hearts are happiest." The words were like a little song that set my seething soul at rest and suddenly made me feel strong. By such a phrase one might feel blest, if weariness enwrapped one quite: "Home-keeping hearts are happiest," this golden phrase would bring delight.

But who shall put the final test? Who is to judge and who construe? "Home-keeping hearts are happiest." Not you for me, nor I for you. For lonely folks with bravest jest may sing as to their work they go: "Home-keeping hearts are happiest"—within the heart the home-fires glow.

Twenty-Seventh Day

MY ESTATE

y friends don't know how rich I am. I'm so discreet, just like a clam; not one of them has e'er been told I own a castle made of gold. My castle's not for sale, don't try! No money in this world could buy this castle with its gardens fair that banish weariness and care.

My castle harbours gentle folks who love to laugh and crack their jokes; the ladies have such flower-like grace and dress in richest silks and lace. This castle stands upon a dream; a fairy built each joist and beam, and Hope's the hostess night and day—she has a most enchanting way!

Fair visions gleam from her two eyes, her mouth is just a sweet surprise, her words are beautiful to hear, they strengthen and they greatly cheer. She is the hostess of this home where ideals have a chance to roam. And now in case you wish to see this palace that enricheth me, perhaps I'd better make it plain—my golden castle is in Spain!

Twenty-Eighth Day

EYES FRONT

"It's looking forward," thus she said, in accents low and quiet breath; "it's ever looking on ahead that keeps the soul from living death." Her words impressed me with their truth. I thought of them again to-day. To look ahead, that is, forsooth, the whole of Nature's noble way.

The tree when bare of bud and leaf looks forward to the Spring again. It has no mind to foster grief because of winter's hostile pain. And when from Nature's lavish breast a fruitful harvest man doth reap, she says with joy, "Now I will rest," and sweetly then she falls asleep.

She must look forward to the time when once again herself she'll give. Oh! it is truer than a rhyme: that by great service do we live. And so I'll give myself away, my brain, my hands, and e'en my heart. And usher in with joy each day, and gladly make a new, fresh start.

Twenty-Ninth Day

NOT FOR ME

he poet pointed to a star: "Ah, that's the way to live, my dear. It dwells remote, so high, so far, no fellow star can interfere." I would not wish to live like that, so far removed from other folks, with no desire to sit and chat nor interchange some starry jokes!

A star I do not wish to be, the very same each single night; I'd rather choke with sympathy or bubble over with delight. I do not wish to live apart a thousand miles from anywhere. Poor star! It hasn't got a heart, and so, of course, it does not care.

So, poet, you may skyward go, if you so please, and live with them; but, as for me, I'll stay below and you can drop a starry gem. I much prefer in crowds to dwell, to jostle with my human kind, and hear home-loving people tell the longings of the heart and mind. I'd rather know a fearful hate that shook my soul till I was sick than have a star's calm, ordered fate: to do a ceaseless twinkling trick!

Thirtieth Day

THE GUEST

h! I must sweep my heart quite clean, take every speck of dust away, and every petty thought and mean, for Joy's to be my guest to-day. Oh! I must fill my heart with song, a happy, lilting, tender lay that banishes all thought of wrong, for Joy's to be my guest to-day.

And honest must my heart's core be, and Kindliness hold it in sway, and love for all humanity, for Joy's to be my guest to-day. My heart must be a tender thing, a creature quite fantastic, gay, uplifted by an unseen wing, for Joy's to be my guest to-day.

My heart must be a quiet place, where Beauty only finds its way; of envy, jealousy, no trace, for Joy's to be my guest to-day. O heart, I beg you show me true when Joy, my guest, arrives to-day, how can I link her fast to you? I want this guest, Sweet Joy, to stay.

Thirty-First Day

THE GRANDPARENTS

At this, the sweetest season of the year, I love to watch, wherever I may be, the grand-dads and the grannies, all so dear, choosing the toys to hang upon the tree.

Oh! watch dear Granny as she makes her choice—a baby doll bedecked with silk and lace—and hear the throb in her maternal voice, and see the look upon her gentle face. Yes, he may laugh at her, this grand-dad tall. It's true she's like a little girl again, hugging her doll, nor does she hear him call, "Now, here's a splendid toy, a model train." Then while with dollies' beds she plays a-space, he crouches low, almost upon the floor, rejoicing in the train's terrific race. There were no toys like these when he was four!

Ah! see them gaze into each other's eyes. Their children's children! Buying toys for them! Such love as theirs the flight of time defies and Happiness gives each her diadem. A charming sight, indeed it is, to see grandparents choosing for the Christmas Tree.

Verses by

WILHELMINA
STITCH

Appear Every Morning
in the

"DAILY GRAPHIC"

Wilhelmina Stitch

The Gift of Day

The very minute I awake,
  I find, and this is every morn,
A precious gift for me to take
  The gift of Day, newborn.

A bowl, translucent, glowing, bright,
  Is this great gift God proffers me,
My hands stretch forth with keen delight
  And clasp it eagerly.

O gift, O precious gift of Day!
  O vessel rare for me to fill!
Let me not stumble on the way,
  I would not use you ill;

But I would fill you to the brim
  With things befitting God's own bowl,
With first a song of praise to Him
  From my most grateful soul.

With all the beauty I can find,
  With flowers that grow along the way,
With tender little deeds and kind,
  With songs and laughter gay.

O heart, be gentle! do not slight
  This gift 'tis yours to use at will;
Then when the shadows fall to-night
  It will be lovely still.

—Wilhelmina Stitch